ROSA ALCHEMICA

SOME GHOST STORIES FROM W. B. YEATS

British Library Cataloguing-in-Publication Data
A catalogue record for this book is available from
the British Library

Contents

THE CURSE OF THE FIRES
AND OF THE SHADOWS

One summer night, when there was peace, a score of Puritan troopers under the pious Sir Frederick Hamilton, broke through the door of the Abbey of the White Friars which stood over the Gara Lough at Sligo. As the door fell with a crash they saw a little knot of friars gathered about the altar, their white habits glimmering in the steady light of the holy candles. All the monks were kneeling except the abbot, who stood upon the altar steps with a great brazen crucifix in his hand. 'Shoot them!' cried Sir Frederick Hamilton, but none stirred, for all were new converts, and feared the crucifix and the holy candles. The white lights from the altar threw the shadows of the troopers up on to roof and wall. As the troopers moved about, the shadows began a fantastic dance among the corbels and the memorial tablets. For a little while all was silent, and then five troopers who were the body-guard of Sir Frederick Hamilton lifted their muskets, and shot down five of the friars. The noise and the smoke drove away the mystery of the pale altar lights, and the other troopers took courage and began to strike. In a moment the friars lay about the altar steps, their white habits stained with blood. 'Set fire to the house!' cried Sir Frederick Hamilton, and at his word one went out, and came in again carrying a heap of dry straw, and piled it against the western wall, and, having done this, fell back, for the fear of the crucifix and of the holy candles was still in his heart. Seeing this, the five troopers who were Sir Frederick Hamilton's body-guard darted forward, and taking each a holy candle set the straw in a blaze. The red tongues of fire rushed up and flickered from corbel to corbel and from tablet to tablet, and crept along the floor, setting in a blaze the seats and benches. The dance of the shadows passed away, and the dance of the fires began. The troopers fell back towards the door in the southern wall, and watched those yellow dancers springing hither and thither.

For a time the altar stood safe and apart in the midst of its white light; the eyes of the troopers turned upon it. The abbot whom they had thought dead had risen to his feet and now stood before it with the crucifix lifted in both hands high above his head. Suddenly he cried with a loud voice, 'Woe unto all who smite those who dwell within the Light of the Lord, for they shall wander among the ungovernable shadows, and follow the ungovernable fires!' And having so cried he fell on his face dead, and the brazen crucifix rolled down the steps of the altar. The smoke had now grown very thick, so that it drove the troopers out into the open air. Before them were burning houses. Behind them shone the painted windows of the Abbey filled with saints and martyrs, awakened, as from a sacred trance, into an angry and animated life. The eyes of the troopers were dazzled, and for a while could see nothing but the flaming faces of saints and martyrs. Presently, however, they saw a man covered with dust who came running towards them. 'Two messengers,' he cried, 'have been sent by the defeated Irish to raise against you the whole country about Manor Hamilton, and if you do not stop them you will be overpowered in the woods before you reach home again! They ride north-east between Ben Bulben and Cashel-na-Gael.'

Sir Frederick Hamilton called to him the five troopers who had first fired upon the monks and said, 'Mount quickly, and ride through the woods towards the mountain, and get before these men, and kill them.'

In a moment the troopers were gone, and before many moments they had splashed across the river at what is now called Buckley's Ford, and plunged into the woods. They followed a beaten track that wound along the northern bank of the river. The boughs of the birch and quicken trees mingled above, and hid the cloudy moonlight, leaving the pathway in almost complete darkness. They rode at a rapid trot, now chatting together, now watching some stray weasel or rabbit scuttling away in the darkness. Gradually, as the gloom and silence of the woods oppressed them, they drew closer together, and began to talk rapidly; they were old comrades and knew each other's lives. One was married, and told how glad his wife would be to see him return safe from this harebrained expedition against the White Friars, and to hear how fortune had made amends for rashness. The oldest of the five, whose wife was dead, spoke of a flagon of wine which awaited him upon an upper shelf; while a third, who was the youngest, had a sweetheart watching for his return, and he rode a little way before the others, not talking at all. Suddenly the young man stopped, and they saw that his horse was trembling. 'I saw something,' he said, 'and yet I do not know but it may have been one of the shadows. It looked like a great worm with a silver crown upon his head.' One of the five put his hand up to his forehead as if about to cross himself, but remembering that he had changed his religion he put it down, and said: 'I am certain it was but a shadow, for there are a great many about us, and of very strange kinds.' Then they rode on in silence. It had been raining in the earlier part of the day, and the drops fell from the branches, wetting their hair and their shoulders. In a little they began to talk again. They had been in many battles against many a rebel together, and now told each other over again the story of their wounds, and so awakened in their hearts the strongest of all fellowships, the fellowship of the sword, and half forgot the terrible solitude of the woods.

Suddenly the first two horses neighed, and then stood still, and would go no further. Before them was a glint of water, and they knew by the rushing sound that it was a river. They dismounted, and after much tugging and coaxing brought the horses to the river-side. In the midst of the water stood a tall old woman with grey hair flowing over a grey dress. She stood up to her knees in the water, and stooped from time to time as though washing. Presently they could see that she was washing something that half floated. The moon cast a flickering light upon it, and they saw that it was the dead body of a man, and, while they were looking at it, an eddy of the river turned the face towards them, and each of the five troopers recognised at the same moment his own face. While they stood dumb and motionless with horror, the woman began to speak, saying slowly and loudly: 'Did you see my son? He has a crown of silver on his head, and there are rubies in the crown.' Then the oldest of the troopers, he who had been most often wounded, drew his sword and cried: 'I have fought for the truth of my God, and need not fear the shadows of Satan,' and with that rushed into the water. In a moment he returned. The woman had vanished, and though he had thrust his sword into air and water he had found nothing.

The five troopers remounted, and set their horses at the ford, but all to no purpose. They tried again and again, and went plunging hither and thither, the horses foaming and rearing. 'Let us,' said the old trooper, 'ride back a little into the wood, and strike the river higher up.' They rode in under the boughs, the ground-ivy crackling under the hoofs, and the branches striking against their steel caps. After about twenty minutes' riding they came out again upon the river, and after another ten minutes found a place where it was possible to cross without sinking below the stirrups. The wood upon the other side was very thin, and broke the moonlight into long streams. The wind had arisen, and had begun to drive the clouds rapidly across the face of the moon, so that thin streams of light seemed to be dancing a grotesque dance among the scattered bushes and small fir-trees. The tops of the trees began also to moan, and the sound of it was like the voice of the dead in the wind; and the troopers remembered the belief that tells how the dead in purgatory are spitted upon the points of the trees and upon the points of the rocks. They turned a little to the south, in the hope that they might strike the beaten path again, but they could find no trace of it.

Meanwhile, the moaning grew louder and louder, and the dance of the white moon-fires more and more rapid. Gradually they began to be aware of a sound of distant music. It was the sound of a bagpipe, and they rode towards it with great joy. It came from the bottom of a deep, cup-like hollow. In the midst of the hollow was an old man with a red cap and withered face. He sat beside a fire of sticks, and had a burning torch thrust into the earth at his feet, and played an old bagpipe furiously. His red hair dripped over his face like the iron rust upon a rock. 'Did you see my wife?' he cried, looking up a moment; 'she was washing! she was washing!' 'I am afraid of him,' said the young trooper, 'I fear he is one of the Sidhe.' 'No,' said the old trooper, 'he is a man, for I can see the sun-freckles upon his face. We will compel him to be our guide;' and at that he drew his sword, and the others did the same. They stood in a ring round the piper, and pointed their swords at him, and the old trooper then told him that they must kill two rebels, who had taken the road between Ben Bulben and the great mountain spur that is called Cashel-na-Gael, and that he must get up before one of them and be their guide, for they had lost their way. The piper turned, and pointed to a neighbouring tree, and they saw an old white horse ready bitted, bridled, and saddled. He slung the pipe across his back, and, taking the torch in his hand, got upon the horse, and started off before them, as hard as he could go.

The wood grew thinner and thinner, and the ground began to slope up toward the mountain. The moon had already set, and the little white flames of the stars had come out everywhere. The ground sloped more and more until at last they rode far above the woods upon the wide top of the mountain. The woods lay spread out mile after mile below, and away to the south shot up the red glare of the burning town. But before and above them were the little white flames. The guide drew rein suddenly, and pointing upwards with the hand that did not hold the torch, shrieked out, 'Look; look at the holy candles!' and then plunged forward at a gallop. waving the torch hither and thither. 'Do you hear the hoofs of the messengers?' cried the guide. 'Quick, quick! or they will be gone out of your hands!' and he laughed as with delight of the chase. The troopers thought they could hear far off, and as if below them, rattle of hoofs; but now the ground began to slope more and more, and the speed grew more headlong moment by moment. They tried to pull up, but in vain, for the horses seemed to have gone mad. The guide had thrown the reins on to the neck of the old white horse, and was waving his arms and singing a wild Gaelic song. Suddenly they saw the thin gleam of a river, at an immense distance below, and knew that they were upon the brink of the abyss that is now called Lug-na-Gael, or in English the Stranger's Leap. The six horses sprang forward, and five screams went up into the air, a moment later five men and horses fell with a dull crash upon the green slopes at the foot of the rocks.

THE WISDOM OF THE KING

*   *   *

The High-Queen of the Island of Woods had died in childbirth,
and her child was put to nurse with a woman who lived in a hut
of mud and wicker, within the border of the wood. One night the

woman sat rocking the cradle, and pondering over the beauty of the child, and praying that the gods might grant him wisdom equal to his beauty. There came a knock at the door, and she got up, not a little wondering, for the nearest neighbours were in the dun of the High-King a mile away; and the night was now late. 'Who is knocking?' she cried, and a thin voice answered, 'Open! for I am a crone of the grey hawk, and I come from the darkness of the great wood.' In terror she drew back the bolt, and a grey-clad woman, of a great age, and of a height more than human, came in and stood by the head of the cradle. The nurse shrank back against the wall, unable to take her eyes from the woman, for she saw by the gleaming of the firelight that the feathers of the grey hawk were upon her head instead of hair. But the child slept, and the fire danced, for the one was too ignorant and the other too full of gaiety to know what a dreadful being stood there. 'Open!' cried another voice, 'for I am a crone of the grey hawk, and I watch over his nest in the darkness of the great wood.' The nurse opened the door again, though her fingers could scarce hold the bolts for trembling, and another grey woman, not less old than the other, and with like feathers instead of hair, came in and stood by the first. In a little, came a third grey woman, and after her a fourth, and then another and another and another, until the hut was full of their immense bodies. They stood a long time in perfect silence and stillness, for they were of those whom the dropping of the sand has never troubled, but at last one muttered in a low thin voice: 'Sisters, I knew him far away by the redness of his heart under his silver skin'; and then another spoke: 'Sisters, I knew him because his heart fluttered like a bird under a net of silver cords'; and then another took up the word: 'Sisters, I knew him because his heart sang like a bird that is happy in a silver cage.'

And after that they sang together, those who were nearest rocking the cradle with long wrinkled fingers; and their voices were now tender and caressing, now like the wind blowing in the great wood, and this was their song:

Out of sight is out of mind:
Long have man and woman-kind,
Heavy of will and light of mood,
Taken away our wheaten food,
Taken away our Altar stone;

8

Hail and rain and thunder alone,
And red hearts we turn to grey,
Are true till Time gutter away.

When the song had died out, the crone who had first spoken, said: 'We have nothing more to do but to mix a drop of our blood into his blood.' And she scratched her arm with the sharp point of a spindle, which she had made the nurse bring to her, and let a drop of blood, grey as the mist, fall upon the lips of the child; and passed out into the darkness. Then the others passed out in silence one by one; and all the while the child had not opened his pink eyelids or the fire ceased to dance, for the one was too ignorant and the other too full of gaiety to know what great beings had bent over the cradle.

When the crones were gone, the nurse came to her courage again, and hurried to the dun of the High-King, and cried out in the midst of the assembly hall that the Sidhe, whether for good or evil she knew not, had bent over the child that night; and the king and his poets and men of law, and his huntsmen, and his cooks, and his chief warriors went with her to the hut and gathered about the cradle, and were as noisy as magpies, and the child sat up and looked at them.

Two years passed over, and the king died fighting against the Fer Bolg; and the poets and the men of law ruled in the name of the child, but looked to see him become the master himself before long, for no one had seen so wise a child, and tales of his endless questions about the household of the gods and the making of the world went hither and thither among the wicker houses of the poor. Everything had been well but for a miracle that began to trouble all men; and all women, who, indeed, talked of it without ceasing. The feathers of the grey hawk had begun to grow in the child's hair, and though his nurse cut them continually, in but a little while they would be more numerous than ever. This had not been a matter of great moment, for miracles were a little thing in those days, but for an ancient law of Eri that none who had any blemish of body could sit upon the throne; and as a grey hawk was a wild thing of the air which had never sat at the board, or listened to the songs of the poets in the light of the fire, it was not possible to think of one in whose hair its feathers grew as other than marred and blasted; nor could the people separate from their admiration of the wisdom that grew in him a horror as at one of unhuman blood.

Yet all were resolved that he should reign, for they had suffered much from foolish kings and their own disorders, and moreover they desired to watch out the spectacle of his days; and no one had any other fear but that his great wisdom might bid him obey the law, and call some other, who had but a common mind, to reign in his stead.

When the child was seven years old the poets and the men of law were called together by the chief poet, and all these matters weighed and considered. The child had already seen that those about him had hair only, and, though they had told him that they too had had feathers but had lost them because of a sin committed by their forefathers, they knew that he would learn the truth when he began to wander into the country round about. After much consideration they decreed a new law commanding every one upon pain of death to mingle artificially the feathers of the grey hawk into his hair; and they sent men with nets and slings and bows into the countries round about to gather a sufficiency of feathers. They decreed also that any who told the truth to the child should be flung from a cliff into the sea.

The years passed, and the child grew from childhood into boyhood and from boyhood into manhood, and from being curious about all things he became busy with strange and subtle thoughts which came to him in dreams, and with distinctions between things long held the same and with the resemblance of things long held different. Multitudes came from other lands to see him and to ask his counsel, but there were guards set at the frontiers, who compelled all that came to wear the feathers of the grey hawk in their hair.

While they listened to him his words seemed to make all darkness light and filled their hearts like music; but, alas, when they returned to their own lands his words seemed far off, and what they could remember too strange and subtle to help them to live out their hasty days. A number indeed did live differently afterwards, but their new life was less excellent than the old: some among them had long served a good cause, but when they heard him praise it and their labour, they returned to their own lands to find what they had loved less lovable and their arm lighter in the battle, for he had taught them how little a hair divides the false and true; others, again, who had served no cause, but wrought in peace the welfare of their own households, when he had expounded the meaning of their purpose, found their bones softer and their will less ready for toil, for he had shown them greater purposes; and numbers of the young, when they had heard him upon all these things, remembered certain words that became like a fire in their hearts, and made all kindly joys and traffic between man and man as nothing, and went different ways, but all into vague regret.

When any asked him concerning the common things of life; disputes about the mear of a territory, or about the straying of cattle, or about the penalty of blood; he would turn to those nearest him for advice; but this was held to be from courtesy, for none knew that these matters were hidden from him by thoughts and dreams that filled his mind like the marching and counter-marching of armies. Far less could any know that his heart wandered lost amid throngs of overcoming thoughts and dreams, shuddering at its own consuming solitude.

Among those who came to look at him and to listen to him was the daughter of a little king who lived a great way off; and when he saw her he loved, for she was beautiful, with a strange and pale beauty unlike the women of his land; but Dana, the great mother, had decreed her a heart that was but as the heart of others, and when she considered the mystery of the hawk feathers she was troubled with a great horror. He called her to him when the assembly was over and told her of her beauty, and praised her simply and frankly as though she were a fable of the bards; and he asked her humbly to give him her love, for he was only subtle in his dreams. Overwhelmed with his greatness, she half consented, and yet half refused, for she longed to marry some warrior who could carry her over a mountain in his arms.

Day by day the king gave her gifts; cups with ears of gold and findrinny wrought by the craftsmen of distant lands; cloth from over sea, which, though woven with curious figures, seemed to her less beautiful than the bright cloth of her own country; and still she was ever between a smile and a frown; between yielding and withholding. He laid down his wisdom at her feet, and told how the heroes when they die return to the world and begin their labour anew; how the kind and mirthful Men of Dea drove out the huge and gloomy and misshapen People from Under the Sea;

and a multitude of things that even the Sidhe have forgotten, either because they happened so long ago or because they have not time to think of them; and still she half refused, and still he hoped, because he could not believe that a beauty so much like wisdom could hide a common heart.

There was a tall young man in the dun who had yellow hair, and was skilled in wrestling and in the training of horses; and one day when the king walked in the orchard, which was between the foss and the forest, he heard his voice among the salley bushes which hid the waters of the foss.

'My blossom,' it said, 'I hate them for making you weave these dingy feathers into your beautiful hair, and all that the bird of prey upon the throne may sleep easy o' nights'; and then the low, musical voice he loved answered: 'My hair is not beautiful like yours; and now that I have plucked the feathers out of your hair I will put my hands through it, thus, and thus, and thus; for it casts no shadow of terror and darkness upon my heart.'

Then the king remembered many things that he had forgotten without understanding them, doubtful words of his poets and his men of law, doubts that he had reasoned away, his own continual solitude; and he called to the lovers in a trembling voice. They came from among the salley bushes and threw themselves at his feet and prayed for pardon, and he stooped down and plucked the feathers out of the hair of the woman and then turned away towards the dun without a word. He strode into the hall of assembly, and having gathered his poets and his men of law about him, stood upon the daïs and spoke in a loud, clear voice:

'Men of law, why did you make me sin against the laws of Eri? Men of verse, why did you make me sin against the secrecy of wisdom, for law was made by man for the welfare of man, but wisdom the gods have made, and no man shall live by its light, for it and the hail and the rain and the thunder follow a way that is deadly to mortal things? Men of law and men of verse, live according to your kind, and call Eocha of the Hasty Mind to reign over you, for I set out to find my kindred.'

He then came down among them, and drew out of the hair of first one and then another the feathers of the grey hawk, and, having scattered them over the rushes upon the floor, passed out, and none dared to follow him, for his eyes gleamed like the eyes of the birds of prey; and no man saw him again or heard his voice.

Some believed that he found his eternal abode among the demons, and some that he dwelt henceforth with the dark and dreadful goddesses, who sit all night about the pools in the forest watching the constellations rising and setting in those desolate mirrors.

Rosa Alchemica

It is now more than ten years since I met, for the last time, Michael
Robartes, and for the first time and the last time his friends and
fellow students; and witnessed his and their tragic end, and endured
those strange experiences, which have changed me so that my
writings have grown less popular and less intelligible, and driven
me almost to the verge of taking the habit of St Dominic. I had
just published *Rosa Alchemica*, a little work on the Alchemists,
somewhat in the manner of Sir Thomas Browne, and had received
many letters from believers in the arcane sciences, upbraiding what
they called my timidity, for they could not believe so evident sympathy but the sympathy of the artist, which is half pity, for everything which has moved men's hearts in any age. I had discovered,
early in my researches, that their doctrine was no merely chemical
phantasy, but a philosophy they applied to the world, to the
elements and to man himself; and that they sought to fashion gold
out of common metals merely as part of an universal transmutation
of all things into some divine and imperishable substance; and this
enabled me to make my little book a fanciful reverie over the
transmutation of life into art, and a cry of measureless desire for
a world made wholly of essences.

I was sitting dreaming of what I had written, in my house in
one of the old parts of Dublin; a house my ancestors had made
almost famous through their part in the politics of the city and
their friendships with the famous men of their generations; and
was feeling an unwonted happiness at having at last accomplished
a long-cherished design, and made my rooms an expression of this
favourite doctrine. The portraits, of more historical than artistic
interest, had gone; and tapestry, full of the blue and bronze of
peacocks, fell over the doors, and shut out all history and activity
untouched with beauty and peace; and now when I looked at my
Crevelli and pondered on the rose in the hand of the Virgin,
wherein the form was so delicate and precise that it seemed more

14

'THE TRUE AND OFFICIAL
ROSICRUCIAN CROSS'

like a thought than a flower, or at the grey dawn and rapturous faces of my Francesca, I knew all a Christian's ecstasy without his slavery to rule and custom; when I pondered over the antique bronze gods and goddesses, which I had mortgaged my house to buy, I had all a pagan's delight in various beauty and without his terror at sleepless destiny and his labour with many sacrifices; and I had only to go to my bookshelf, where every book was bound in leather, stamped with intricate ornament, and of a carefully chosen colour: Shakespeare in the orange of the glory of the world, Dante in the dull red of his anger, Milton in the blue-grey of his formal calm; and I could experience what I would of human passions without their bitterness and without satiety. I had gathered about me all gods because I believed in none, and experienced every pleasure because I gave myself to none, but held myself apart, individual, indissoluble, a mirror of polished steel: I looked in the triumph of this imagination at the birds of Hera, glowing in the firelight as though they were wrought of jewels; and to my mind, for which symbolism was a necessity, they seemed the doorkeepers of my world, shutting out all that was not of as affluent a beauty as their own; and for a moment I thought as I had thought in so many other moments, that it was possible to rob life of every bitterness except the bitterness of death; and then a thought which had followed this thought, time after time, filled me with a passionate sorrow. All those forms: that Madonna with her brooding purity, those rapturous faces singing in the morning light, those bronze divinities with their passionless dignity, those wild shapes rushing from despair to despair, belonged to a divine world wherein I had no part; and every experience, however profound, every perception, however exquisite, would bring me the bitter dream of a limitless energy I could never know, and even in my most perfect moment I would be two selves, the one watching with heavy eyes the other's moment of content. I had heaped about me the gold born in the crucibles of others; but the supreme dream of the alchemist, the transmutation of the weary heart into a weariless spirit, was as far from me as, I doubted not, it had been from him also. I turned to my last purchase, a set of alchemical apparatus which, the dealer in the Rue le Peletier had assured me, once belonged to Raymond Lully, and as I joined the *alembic* to the *athanor* and laid the *lavacrum maris* at their side, I understood the alchemical doctrine, that all beings, divided from the great deep where spirits wander, one and yet a multitude, are weary; and sympathised, in the pride of my connoisseurship, with the consuming thirst for destruction which made the alchemist veil under his symbols of lions and dragons, of eagles and ravens, of dew and of nitre, a search for an essence which would dissolve all mortal things. I repeated to myself the ninth key of Basilius Valentinus, in which he compares the fire of the last day to the fire of the alchemist, and the world to the alchemist's furnace, and would have us know that all must be dissolved before the divine substance, material gold or immaterial ecstasy, awake. I had dissolved indeed the mortal world and lived amid immortal essences, but had obtained no miraculous ecstasy. As I thought of these things, I drew aside the curtains and looked out into the darkness, and it seemed to my troubled fancy that all those little points of light filling the sky were the furnaces of innumerable divine alchemists, who labour continually, turning lead into gold, weariness into ecstasy, bodies into souls, the darkness into God; and at their perfect labour my mortality grew heavy, and I cried out, as so many dreamers and men of letters in our age have cried, for the birth of that elaborate spiritual beauty which could alone uplift souls weighted with so many dreams.

My reverie was broken by a loud knocking at the door, and I wondered the more at this because I had no visitors, and had bid my servants do all things silently, lest they broke the dream of my inner life. Feeling a little curious, I resolved to go to the door myself, and, taking one of the silver candlesticks from the mantelpiece, began to descend the stairs. The servants appeared to be out, for though the sound poured through every corner and crevice of the house there was no stir in the lower rooms. I remembered that because my needs were so few, my part in life so little, they had begun to come and go as they would, often leaving me alone for hours. The emptiness and silence of a world from which I had driven everything but dreams suddenly overwhelmed me, and I shuddered as I drew the bolt. I found before me Michael Robartes, whom I had not seen for years, and whose wild red hair, fierce eyes, sensitive, tremulous lips and rough clothes made him look now, just as they used to do fifteen years before, something between a debauchee, a saint, and a peasant. He had recently come to Ireland, he said, and wished to see me on a matter of importance; indeed, the only matter of importance for him and for me. His voice brought up before me our student years in Paris, and remembering the magnetic power he had once possessed over me, a little fear mingled with much annoyance at this irrelevant intrusion, as I led the way up the wide staircase, where Swift had passed joking and railing, and Curran telling stories and quoting Greek, in simpler days, before men's minds, subtilised and complicated by the romantic movement in art and literature, began to tremble on the verge of some unimagined revelation. I felt that my hand shook, and saw that the light of the candle wavered and quivered more than it need have upon the Maenads on the old French panels, making them look like the first beings slowly shaping in the formless and void darkness. When the door had closed, and the peacock curtain, glimmering like many-coloured flame, fell between us and the world, I felt, in a way I could not understand, that some singular and unexpected thing was about to happen. I went over to the mantelpiece, and finding that a little chainless bronze censer, set, upon the outside, with pieces of painted china by Orazio

Fontana, which I had filled with antique amulets, had fallen upon its side and poured out its contents, I began to gather the amulets into the bowl, partly to collect my thoughts and partly with that habitual reverence which seemed to me the due of things so long connected with secret hopes and fears. 'I see,' said Michael Robartes, 'that you are still fond of incense, and I can show you an incense more precious than any you have ever seen,' and as he spoke he took the censer out of my hand and put the amulets in a little heap between the *athanor* and the *alembic*. I sat down, and he sat down at the side of the fire, and sat there for a while looking into the fire, and holding the censer in his hand. 'I have come to ask you something,' he said, 'and the incense will fill the room, and our thoughts, with its sweet odour while we are talking. I got it from an old man in Syria, who said it was made from flowers, of one kind with the flowers that laid their heavy purple petals upon the hands and upon the hair and upon the feet of Christ in the Garden of Gethsemane, and folded Him in their heavy breath, until He cried against the cross and his destiny.' He shook some dust into the censer out of a small silk bag, and set the censer upon the floor and lit the dust which sent up a blue stream of smoke, that spread out over the ceiling, and flowed downwards again until it was like Milton's banyan tree. It filled me, as incense often does, with a faint sleepiness, so that I started when he said, 'I have come to ask you that question which I asked you in Paris, and which you left Paris rather than answer.'

He had turned his eyes towards me, and I saw them glitter in the firelight, and through the incense, as I replied : 'You mean, will I become an initiate of your Order of the Alchemical Rose? I would not consent in Paris, when I was full of unsatisfied desire, and now that I have at last fashioned my life according to my desire, am I likely to consent?'

'You have changed greatly since then,' he answered. 'I have read your books, and now I see you among all these images, and I understand you better than you do yourself, for I have been with many and many dreamers at the same cross-ways. You have shut away the world and gathered the gods about you, and if you do not throw yourself at their feet, you will be always full of lassitude, and of wavering purpose, for a man must forget he is miserable in the bustle and noise of the multitude in this world and in time; or seek a mystical union with the multitude who govern this world and time.' And then he murmured something I could not hear, and as though to someone I could not see.

For a moment the room appeared to darken, as it used to do when he was about to perform some singular experiment, and in the darkness the peacocks upon the doors seemed to glow with a more intense colour. I cast off the illusion, which was, I believe, merely caused by memory, and by the twilight of incense, for I would not acknowledge that he could overcome my now mature intellect; and I said : 'Even if I grant that I need a spiritual belief and some form of worship, why should I go to Eleusis and not to Calvary?' He leaned forward and began speaking with a slightly rhythmical intonation, and as he spoke I had to struggle again with the shadow, as of some older night than the night of the sun, which began to dim the light of the candles and to blot out the little gleams upon the corner of picture-frames and on the bronze divinities, and to turn the blue of the incense to a heavy purple; while it left the peacocks to glimmer and glow as though each separate colour were a living spirit. I had fallen into a profound dream-like reverie in which I heard him speaking as at a distance. 'And yet there is no one who communes with only one god,' he was saying, 'and the more a man lives in imagination and in a refined understanding, the more gods does he meet with and talk with, and the more does he come under the power of Roland, who sounded in the Valley of Roncesvalles the last trumpet of the body's will and pleasure; and of Hamlet, who saw them perishing away, and sighed; and of Faust, who looked for them up and down the world and could not find them; and under the power of all those countless divinities who have taken upon themselves spiritual bodies in the minds of the modern poets and romance writers, and under the power of the old divinities, who since the Renaissance have won everything of their ancient worship except the sacrifice of birds and fishes, the fragrance of garlands and the smoke of incense. The many think humanity made these divinities, and that it can unmake them again; but we who have seen them pass in rattling harness, and in soft robes, and heard them speak with articulate voices while we lay in deathlike trance, know that they are always making and unmaking humanity, which is indeed but the trembling of their lips.'

He had stood up and begun to walk to and fro, and had become in my waking dream a shuttle weaving an immense purple web

whose folds had begun to fill the room. The room seemed to have
become inexplicably silent, as though all but the web and the
weaving were at an end in the world. 'They have come to us; they
have come to us,' the voice began again; 'all that have ever been
in your reverie, all that you have met with in books. There is Lear,
his head still wet with the thunder-storm, and he laughs because
you thought yourself an existence who are but a shadow, and him
a shadow who is an eternal god; and there is Beatrice, with her
lips half parted in a smile, as though all the stars were about to
pass away in a sigh of love; and there is the mother of the God of
humility who cast so great a spell over men that they have
tried to un-people their hearts that he might reign alone,
but she holds in her hand the rose whose every petal is a
god; and there, O swiftly she comes! is Aphrodite under a twilight
falling from the wings of numberless sparrows, and about her feet
are the grey and white doves.' In the midst of my dream I saw
him hold out his left arm and pass his right hand over it as though
he stroked the wings of doves. I made a violent effort which seemed
almost to tear me in two, and said with forced determination :
'You would sweep me away into an indefinite world which fills me
with terror; and yet a man is a great man just in so far as he can
make his mind reflect everything with indifferent precision like a
mirror.' I seemed to be perfectly master of myself, and went on,
but more rapidly : 'I command you to leave me at once, for your
ideas and phantasies are but the illusions that creep like maggots
into civilisations when they begin to decline, and into minds when
they begin to decay.' I had grown suddenly angry, and seizing the
alembic from the table, was about to rise and strike him with it,
when the peacocks on the door behind him appeared to grow
immense; and then the *alembic* fell from my fingers and I was
drowned in a tide of green and blue and bronze feathers, and as I
struggled hopelessly I heard a distant voice saying : 'Our master
Avicenna has written that all life proceeds out of corruption.' The
glittering feathers had now covered me completely, and I knew
that I had struggled for hundreds of years, and I was conquered at
last. I was sinking into the depth when the green and blue and
bronze that seemed to fill the world became a sea of flame and
swept me away, and as I was swirled along I heard a voice over
my head cry, 'The mirror is broken in two pieces,' and another
voice answer, 'The mirror is broken in four pieces,' and a more

distant voice cry with an exultant cry, 'The mirror is broken into numberless pieces'; and then a multitude of pale hands were reaching towards me, and strange gentle faces bending above me, and half wailing and half caressing voices uttering words that were forgotten the moment they were spoken. I was being lifted out of the tide of flame, and felt my memories, my hopes, my thoughts, my will, everything I held to be myself, melting away; then I seemed to rise through numberless companies of beings who were, I understood, in some way more certain than thought, each wrapped in his eternal moment, in the perfect lifting of an arm, in a little circlet of rhythmical words, in dreaming with dim eyes and half-closed eyelids. And then I passed beyond these forms, which were so beautiful they had almost ceased to be, and, having endured strange moods, melancholy, as it seemed, with the weight of many worlds, I passed into that Death which is Beauty herself, and into that Loneliness which all the multitudes desire without ceasing. All things that had ever lived seemed to come and dwell in my heart, and I in theirs; and I had never again known mortality or tears, had I not suddenly fallen from the certainty of vision into the uncertainty of dream, and become a drop of molten gold falling with immense rapidity, through a night elaborate with stars, and all about me a melancholy exultant wailing. I fell and fell and fell, and then the wailing was but the wailing of the wind in the chimney, and I awoke to find myself leaning upon the table and supporting my head with my hands. I saw the *alembic* swaying from side to side in the distant corner it had rolled to, and Michael Robartes watching me and waiting. 'I will go wherever you will,' I said, 'and do whatever you bid me, for I have been with eternal things.' 'I knew,' he replied, 'you must need answer as you have answered, when I heard the storm begin. You must come to a great distance, for we were commanded to build our temple between the pure multitude by the waves and the impure multitude of men.'

III

I did not speak as we drove through the deserted streets, for my mind was curiously empty of familiar thoughts and experiences; it seemed to have been plucked out of the definite world and cast naked upon a shoreless sea. There were moments when the vision appeared on the point of returning, and I would half-remember, with an ecstasy of joy or sorrow, crimes and heroisms, fortunes and misfortunes; or begin to contemplate, with a sudden leaping of the heart, hopes and terrors, desires and ambitions, alien to my orderly and careful life; and then I would awake shuddering at the thought that some great imponderable being had swept through my mind. It was indeed days before this feeling passed perfectly away, and even now, when I have sought refuge in the only definite faith, I feel a great tolerance for those people with incoherent personalities, who gather in the chapels and meeting-places of certain obscure sects, because I also have felt fixed habits and principles dissolving before a power, which was *hysterica passio* or sheer madness, if you will, but was so powerful in its melancholy exultation that I tremble lest it wake again and drive me from my new-found peace.

When we came in the grey light to the great half-empty terminus, it seemed to me I was so changed that I was no more, as man is, a moment shuddering at eternity, but eternity weeping and laughing over a moment; and when we had started and Michael Robartes had fallen asleep, as he soon did, his sleeping face, in which there was no sign of all that had so shaken me and that now kept me wakeful, was to my excited mind more like a mask than a face. The fancy possessed me that the man behind it had dissolved away like salt in water, and that it laughed and sighed, appealed and denounced at the bidding of beings greater or less than man. 'This is not Michael Robartes at all : Michael Robartes is dead; dead for ten, for twenty years perhaps,' I kept repeating to myself. I fell at last into a feverish sleep, waking up from time to time when we rushed past some little town, its slated roofs shining with wet, or still lake gleaming in the cold morning light. I had been too preoccupied to ask where we were going, or to notice what tickets Michael Robartes had taken, but I knew now from the direction of the sun that we were going westward; and presently I knew also, by the way in which the trees had grown into the semblance of tattered beggars flying with bent heads towards the east, that we were approaching the western coast. Then immediately I saw the sea between the low hills upon the left, its dull grey broken into white patches and lines.

When we left the train we had still, I found, some way to go, and set out, buttoning our coats about us, for the wind was bitter and violent. Michael Robartes was silent, seeming anxious to leave me to my thoughts; and as we walked between the sea and the rocky side of a great promontory, I realised with a new perfection what a shock had been given to all my habits of thought and of feelings, if indeed some mysterious change had not taken place in the substance of my mind, for the grey waves, plumed with scudding foam, had grown part of a teeming, fantastic inner life; and when Michael Robartes pointed to a square ancient-looking house, with a much smaller and newer building under its lee, set out on the very end of a dilapidated and almost deserted pier, and said it was the Temple of the Alchemical Rose, I was possessed with the phantasy that the sea, which kept covering it with showers of white foam, was claiming it as part of some indefinite and passionate life, which had begun to war upon our orderly and careful days, and was about to plunge the world into a night as obscure as that which followed the downfall of the classical world. One part of my mind mocked this phantastic terror, but the other, the part that still lay half plunged in vision, listened to the clash of unknown armies, and shuddered at unimaginable fanaticisms, that hung in those grey leaping waves.

We had gone but a few paces along the pier when we came upon an old man, who was evidently a watchman, for he sat in an overset barrel, close to a place where masons had been lately working upon a break in the pier, and had in front of him a fire such as one sees slung under tinkers' carts. I saw that he was also a voteen, as the peasants say, for there was a rosary hanging from a nail on the rim of the barrel, and as I saw I shuddered, and I did not know why I shuddered. We had passed him a few yards when I heard him cry in Gaelic, 'Idolaters, idolaters, go down to Hell with your witches and your devils; go down to Hell that the herrings may come again into the bay'; and for some moments I could hear him half screaming and half muttering behind us. 'Are you not afraid,' I said, 'that these wild fishing people may do some desperate thing against you?'

'I and mine,' he answered, 'are long past human hurt or help, being incorporate with immortal spirits, and when we die it shall be the consummation of the supreme work. A time will come for these people also, and they will sacrifice a mullet to Artemis, or some other fish to some new divinity, unless indeed their own divinities, the Dagda, with his overflowing cauldron, Lug, with his spear dipped in poppy-juice lest it rush forth hot for battle, Aengus, with the three birds on his shoulder, Bodb and his red swineherd, and all the heroic children of Dana, set up once more their temples of grey stone. Their reign has never ceased, but only waned in power a little, for the Sidhe still pass in every wind, and dance and play at hurley, and fight their sudden battles in every hollow and on every hill; but they cannot build their temples again till there have been martyrdoms and victories, and perhaps even that long-foretold battle in the Valley of the Black Pig.'

Keeping close to the wall that went about the pier on the sea-ward side, to escape the driving foam and the wind, which threat-ened every moment to lift us off our feet, we made our way in silence to the door of the square building. Michael Robartes opened it with a key, on which I saw the rust of many salt winds, and led me along a bare passage and up an uncarpeted stair to a little room surrounded with bookshelves. A meal would be brought, but only of fruit, for I must submit to a tempered fast before the ceremony, he explained, and with it a book on the doctrine and method of the Order, over which I was to spend what remained of the winter daylight. He then left me, promising to return an hour before the ceremony. I began searching among the bookshelves, and found one of the most exhaustive alchemical libraries I have ever seen. There were the works of Morienus, who hid his immortal body under a shirt of hair-cloth; of Avicenna, who was a drunkard and yet controlled numberless legions of spirits; of Alfarabi, who put so many spirits into his lute that he could make men laugh, or weep, or fall in deadly trance as he would; of Lully, who trans-formed himself into the likeness of a red cock; of Flamel, who with his wife Parnella achieved the elixir many hundreds of years ago, and is fabled to live still in Arabia among the Dervishes; and of many of less fame. There were very few mystics but alchemical mystics, and because, I had little doubt, of the devotion to one god of the greater number and of the limited sense of beauty, which Robartes would hold an inevitable consequence; but I did notice a complete set of facsimiles of the prophetical writings of William Blake, and probably because of the multitudes that thronged his illumination and were 'like the gay fishes on the wave when the moon sucks up the dew.' I noted also many poets and prose writers of every age, but only those who were a little weary of life, as indeed the greatest have been everywhere, and who cast their imagination to us, as a something they needed no longer now that they were going up in their fiery chariots.

Presently I heard a tap at the door, and a woman came in and laid a little fruit upon the table. I judged that she had once been handsome, but her cheeks were hollowed by what I would have held, had I seen her anywhere else, an excitement of the flesh and a thirst for pleasure, instead of which it doubtless was an excitement of the imagination and a thirst for beauty. I asked her some question concerning the ceremony, but getting no answer except a shake of the head, saw that I must await initiation in silence. When I had eaten, she came again, and having laid a curiously wrought bronze box on the table, lighted the candles, and took away the plates and the remnants. So soon as I was alone, I turned to the box, and found that the peacocks of Hera spread out their tails over the sides and lid, against a background, on which were wrought great stars, as though to affirm that the heavens were a part of their glory. In the box was a book bound in vellum, and having upon the vellum and in very delicate colours, and in gold, the alchemical rose with many spears thrusting against it, but in vain, as was shown by the shattered points of those nearest to the petals. The book was written upon vellum, and in beautiful clear letters, interspersed with symbolical pictures and illuminations, after the manner of the *Splendor Solis*.

The first chapter described how six students, of Celtic descent, gave themselves separately to the study of alchemy, and solved, one the mystery of the Pelican, another the mystery of the green Dragon, another the mystery of the Eagle, another that of Salt and Mercury. What seemed a succession of accidents, but was, the book declared, the contrivance of preternatural powers, brought them together in the garden of an inn in the South of France, and while they talked together the thought came to them that alchemy was the gradual distillation of the contents of the soul, until they were ready to put off the mortal and put on the immortal. An owl passed, rustling among the vine-leaves over-head, and then an old woman came, leaning upon a stick, and, sitting close to them, took up the thought where they had dropped it. Having expounded the whole principle of spiritual alchemy, and bid them found the Order of the Alchemical Rose, she passed from among them, and when they would have followed was nowhere to be seen. They formed themselves into an Order, holding their goods and making their researches in common, and, as they became perfect in the alchemical doctrine, apparitions came and went among them, and taught them more and more marvellous mysteries. The book then went on to expound so much of these as the neophyte was permitted to know, dealing at the outset and at considerable length with the independent reality of our thoughts, which was, it declared, the doctrine from which all true doctrines rose. If you imagine, it said, the semblance of a living being, it is at once possessed by a wandering soul, and goes hither and thither working good or evil, until the moment of its death has come; and gave many examples, received, it said, from many gods. Eros had taught them how to fashion forms in which a divine soul could dwell, and whisper what they would into sleeping minds; and Ate, forms from which demonic beings could pour madness, or unquiet dreams, into sleeping blood; and Hermes, that if you powerfully imagined a hound at your bedside it would keep watch there until you woke, and drive away all but the mightiest demons, but that if your imagination was weakly, the hound would be weakly also, and the demons prevail, and the hound soon die; and Aphrodite, that if you made, by a strong imagining, a dove crowned with silver and had it flutter over your head, its soft cooing would make sweet dreams of immortal love gather and brood over mortal sleep; and all divinities alike had revealed with many warnings and lamentations that all minds are continually giving birth to such beings, and sending them forth to work health or disease, joy or madness. If you would give forms to the evil powers, it went on, you were to make them ugly, thrusting out a lip, with the thirsts of life, or breaking the proportions of a body with the burdens of life; but the divine powers would only appear in beautiful shapes, which are but, as it were, shapes trembling out of existence, folding up into a timeless ecstasy, drifting with half-shut eyes, into a sleepy stillness. The bodiless souls who descended into these forms were what men call the moods; and worked all great changes in the world; for just as the magician or the artist could call them when he would, so they could call out of the mind of the magician or the artist, or if they were demons, out of the mind of the mad or the ignoble, what shape they would, and through its voice and its gestures pour themselves out upon the world. In this way all great events were accomplished; a mood, a divinity, or a demon, first descending like a faint sigh into men's minds and then changing their thoughts and their actions until hair that was yellow had grown black, or hair that was black had grown yellow, and empires moved their border, as though they were but drifts of leaves. The rest of the book contained symbols of form, and sound, and colour, and their attribution to divinities and demons, so that the initiate might fashion a shape for any divinity or any demon, and be as powerful as Avicenna among those who live under the roots of tears and of laughter.

IV

A couple of hours after sunset Michael Robartes returned and told me that I would have to learn the steps of an exceedingly antique dance because before my initiation could be perfected I had to join three times in a magical dance, for rhythm was the wheel of Eternity, on which alone the transient and accidental could be broken, and the spirit set free. I found that the steps, which were simple enough, resembled certain antique Greek dances, and having been a good dancer in my youth and the master of many curious Gaelic steps, I soon had them in my memory. He then robed me and himself in a costume which suggested by its shape both Greece and Egypt, but by its crimson colour a more passionate life than theirs; and having put into my hands a little chainless censer of bronze, wrought into the likeness of a rose, by some modern crafts-man, he told me to open a small door opposite to the door by which I had entered. I put my hand to the handle, but the moment I did so the fumes of the incense, helped perhaps by his mysterious glamour, made me fall again into a dream, in which I seemed to be a mask, lying on the counter of a little Eastern shop. Many persons, with eyes so bright and still that I knew them for more than human, came in and tried me on their faces, but at last flung me into a corner with a little laughter; but all this passed in a moment, for when I awoke my hand was still upon the handle. I opened the door, and found myself in a marvellous passage, along whose sides were many divinities wrought in a mosaic, not less beautiful than the mosaic in the Baptistery at Ravenna, but of a less severe beauty; the predominant colour of each divinity, which was surely a symbolic colour, being repeated in the lamps that hung from the ceiling, a curiously-scented lamp before every divinity. I passed on, marvelling exceedingly how these enthusiasts could have created all this beauty in so remote a place, and half persuaded to believe in a material alchemy, by the sight of so much hidden wealth; the censer filling the air, as I passed, with smoke of ever-changing colour.

I stopped before a door, on whose bronze panels were wrought great waves in whose shadows were faint suggestions of terrible faces. Those beyond it seemed to have heard our steps, for a voice cried: 'Is the work of the Incorruptible Fire at an end?' and immediately Michael Robartes answered: 'The perfect gold has come from the *athanor*.' The door swung open, and we were in a great circular room, and among men and women who were dancing slowly in crimson robes. Upon the ceiling was an immense rose wrought in mosaic; and about the walls, also in mosaic, was a battle of gods and angels, the gods glimmering like rubies and sapphires, and the angels of the one greyness, because, as Michael Robartes whispered, they had renounced their divinity, and turned from the unfolding of their separate hearts, out of love for a God of humility and sorrow. Pillars supported the roof and made a kind of circular cloister, each pillar being a column of confused shapes, divinities, it seemed, of the wind, who rose as in a whirling dance of more than human vehemence, and playing upon pipes and cymbals; and from among these shapes were thrust out hands, and in these hands were censers. I was bid place my censer also in a hand and take my place and dance, and as I turned from the pillars towards the dancers, I saw that the floor was of a green stone, and that a pale Christ on a pale cross was wrought in the midst. I asked Robartes the meaning of this, and was told that they desired 'To trouble His unity with their mul-titudinous feet.' The dance wound in and out, tracing upon the floor the shapes of petals that copied the petals in the rose overhead, and to the sound of hidden instruments which were perhaps of an antique pattern, for I have never heard the like; and every moment the dance was more passionate, until all the winds of the world seemed to have awakened under our feet. After a little I had grown weary, and stood under a pillar watching the coming and going of those flame-like figures; until gradually I sank into a half-dream, from which I was awakened by seeing the petals of the great rose, which had no longer the look of mosaic, falling slowly through the incense-heavy air, and, as they fell, shaping into the likeness of living my soul as an ox drinks up a wayside pool; and I fell, and darkness passed over me.

V

I awoke suddenly as though something had awakened me, and saw that I was lying on a roughly painted floor, and that on the ceiling, which was at no great distance, was a roughly painted rose, and about me on the walls half-finished paintings. The pillars and the censers had gone; and near me a score of sleepers lay wrapped in disordered robes, their upturned faces looking to my imagination like hollow masks; and a chill dawn was shining down upon them from a long window I had not noticed before; and outside the sea roared. I saw Michael Robartes lying at a little distance and beside him an overset bowl of wrought bronze which looked as though it had once held incense. As I sat thus, I heard a sudden tumult of angry men's and women's voices mix with the roaring of the sea; and leaping to my feet, I went quickly to Michael Robartes, and tried to shake him out of his sleep. I then seized him by the shoulder and tried to lift him, but he fell backwards, and sighed faintly; and the voices became louder and angrier; and there was a sound of heavy blows upon the door, which opened on to the pier. Suddenly I heard a sound of rending wood, and I knew it had begun to give, and I ran to the door of the room. I pushed it open and came out upon a passage whose bare boards clattered under my feet, and found in the passage another door which led into an empty kitchen; and as I passed through the door I heard two crashes in quick succession, and knew by the sudden noise of feet and the shouts that the door which opened on to the pier had fallen inwards. I ran from the kitchen and out into a small yard, and from this down some steps which descended the seaward and sloping side of the pier, and from the steps clambered along the water's edge, with the angry voices ringing in my ears. This part of the pier had been but lately refaced with blocks of granite, so that it was almost clear of seaweed; but when I came to the old part, I found it so slippery with green weed that I had to climb up on to the roadway. I looked towards the Temple of the Alchemical Rose, where the fishermen and the women were still shouting, but somewhat more faintly, and saw that there was no one about the door or upon

29

the pier; but as I looked, a little crowd hurried out of the door and began gathering large stones from where they were heaped up in readiness for the next time a storm shattered the pier, when they would be laid under blocks of granite. While I stood watching the crowd, an old man, who was, I think, the voteen, pointed to me, and screamed out something, and the crowd whitened, for all the faces had turned towards me. I ran, and it was well for me that pullers of the oar are poorer men with their feet than with their arms and their bodies; and yet while I ran I scarcely heard the following feet or the angry voices, for many voices of exultation and lamentation, which were forgotten as a dream is forgotten the moment they were heard, seemed to be ringing in the air over my head.

There are moments even now when I seem to hear those voices of exultation and lamentation, and when the indefinite world, which has but half lost its mastery over my heart and my intellect, seems about to claim a perfect mastery; but I carry the rosary about my neck, and when I hear, or seem to hear them, I press it to my heart and say: 'He whose name is Legion is at our doors deceiving our intellects with subtlety and flattering our hearts with beauty, and we have no trust but in Thee'; and then the war that rages within me at other times is still, and I am at peace.

beings of an extraordinary beauty. Still faint and cloud-like, they began to dance, and as they danced took a more and more definite shape, so that I was able to distinguish beautiful Grecian faces and august Egyptian faces, and now and again to name a divinity by the staff in his hand or by a bird fluttering over his head; and soon every mortal foot danced by the white foot of an immortal; and in the troubled eyes that looked into untroubled shadowy eyes, I saw the brightness of uttermost desire as though they had found at length, after unreckonable wandering, the lost love of their youth. Sometimes, but only for a moment, I saw a faint solitary figure with a veiled face, and carrying a faint torch, flit among the dancers, but like a dream within a dream, like a shadow of a shadow, and I knew by an understanding born from a deeper fountain than thought, that it was Eros himself, and that his face was veiled because no man or woman from the beginning of the world has ever known what love is, or looked into his eyes, for Eros alone of divinities is altogether a spirit, and hides in passions not of his essence if he would commune with a mortal heart. So that if a man love nobly he knows love through infinite pity, unspeakable trust, unending sympathy; and if ignobly through vehement jealousy, sudden hatred, and unappeasable desire; but unveiled love he never knows. While I thought these things, a voice cried to me from the crimson figures: 'Into the dance! there is none that can be spared out of the dance; into the dance! into the dance! that the gods may make them bodies out of the substance of our hearts'; and before I could answer, a mysterious wave of passion, that seemed like the soul of the dance moving within our souls, took hold of me, and I was swept, neither consenting nor refusing, into the midst. I was dancing with an immortal august woman, who had black lilies in her hair, and her dreamy gesture seemed laden with a wisdom more profound than the darkness that is between star and star, and with a love like the love that breathed upon the waters; and as we danced on and on, the incense drifted over us and round us, covering us away as in the heart of the world, and ages seemed to pass, and tempests to awake and perish in the folds of our robes and in her heavy hair.

Suddenly I remembered that her eyelids had never quivered, and that her lilies had not dropped a black petal, or shaken from their places, and understood with a great horror that I danced with one who was more or less than human, and who was drinking up

31

THE SORCERERS

*

In Ireland we hear but little of the darker powers,* and come across any who have seen them even more rarely, for the imagination of the people dwells rather upon the fantastic and capricious, and fantasy and caprice would lose the freedom which is their breath of life, were they to unite them either with evil or with good. I have indeed come across very few persons in Ireland who try to communicate with evil powers, and the few I have met keep their purpose and practice wholly hidden from those among whom they live. They are mainly small clerks, and meet for the purpose of their art in a room hung with black hangings, but in what town that room is I shall not say. They would not admit me into this room, but finding me not altogether ignorant of the arcane science, showed elsewhere what they could do. 'Come to us,' said their leader, 'and we will show you spirits who will talk to you face to face, and in shapes as solid and heavy as our own.'

I had been talking of the power of communicating in states of trance with the angelical and faery beings, – the children of

*I know better now. We have the dark powers much more than I thought, but not as much as the Scottish, and yet I think the imagination of the people does dwell chiefly upon the fantastic and capricious.

the day and of the twilight; – and he had been contending that we should only believe in what we can see and feel when in our ordinary everyday state of mind. 'Yes,' I said, 'I will come to you,' or some such words; 'but I will not permit myself to become entranced, and will therefore know whether these shapes you talk of are any the more to be touched and felt by the ordinary senses than are those I talk of.' I was not denying the power of other beings to take upon themselves a clothing of mortal substance, but only that simple invocations, such as he spoke of, seemed unlikely to do more than cast the mind into trance.

'But,' he said, 'we have seen them move the furniture hither and thither, and they go at our bidding, and help or harm people who know nothing of them.' I am not giving the exact words, but as accurately as I can the substance of our talk.

On the night arranged I turned up about eight, and found the leader sitting alone in almost total darkness in a small back room. He was dressed in a black gown, like an inquisitor's dress in an old drawing, that left nothing of him visible except his eyes, which peered out through two small round holes. Upon the table in front of him was a brass dish of burning herbs, a large bowl, a skull covered with painted symbols, two crossed daggers, and certain implements, whose use I failed to discover, shaped like quern stones. I also put on a black gown, and remember that it did not fit perfectly, and that it interfered with my movements considerably. The sorcerer then took a black cock out of a basket, and cut its throat with one of the daggers, letting the blood fall into the large bowl. He opened a book and began an invocation, which was neither English nor Irish, and had a deep guttural sound. Before he had finished, another of the sorcerers, a man of about twenty-five, came in, and having put on a black gown also, seated himself at my left hand. I had the invoker directly in front of me, and soon began to find his eyes, which glittered through the small holes in his hood, affecting me in a cruious way. I struggled hard against their influence, and my head began to ache. The invocation continued, and nothing happened for the first few minutes. Then the invoker got up and extinguished the light in the hall, so that no glimmer might come through the slit under the door. There was now no light except from the herbs on the brass dish, and no sound except from the deep guttural murmur of the invocation.

Presently the man at my left swayed himself about, and cried out, 'O god! O god!' I asked him what ailed him, but he did not know he had spoken. A moment after he said he could see a great serpent moving about the room, and became considerably excited. I saw nothing with any definite shape, but thought that black clouds were forming about me. I felt I must fall into a trance if I did not struggle against it, and that the influence which was causing this trance was out of harmony with itself, in other words, evil. After a struggle I got rid of the black clouds, and was able to observe with my ordinary senses again. The two sorcerers now began to see black and white columns moving about the room, and finally a man in a monk's habit, and they became greatly puzzled because I did not see these things also, for to them they were as solid as the table before them. The invoker appeared to be gradually increasing in power, and I began to feel as if a tide of darkness was pouring from him and concentrating itself about me; and now too I noticed that the man on my left hand had passed into a death-like trance. With a last great effort I drove off the black clouds; but feeling them to be the only shapes I could see without passing into a trance, and having no great love for them, I asked for lights, and after the needful exorcism returned to the ordinary world.

I said to the more powerful of the two sorcerers, 'What would happen if one of your spirits had overpowered me?' 'You would go out of this room,' he answered, 'with his character added to your own.' I asked about the origin of his sorcery, but got little of importance, except that he had learned it from his father, and that one word which he had repeated several times was Arabic. He would not tell me more, for he had, it appeared, taken a vow of secrecy.

THE CRUCIFIXION OF THE OUTCAST

A man, with thin brown hair and a pale face, half ran, half walked, along the road that wound from the south to the town of Sligo. Many called him Cumhal, the son of Cormac, and many called him the Swift, Wild Horse; and he was a gleeman, and he wore a short parti-coloured doublet, and had pointed shoes, and a bulging wallet. Also he was of the blood of the Ernaans, and his birthplace was the Field of Gold; but his eating and sleeping places were in the five kingdoms of Eri, and his abiding place was not upon the ridge of the earth. His eyes strayed from the tower of what was later the Abbey of the White Friars to a row of crosses which stood out against the sky upon a hill a little to the eastward of the town, and he clenched his fist, and shook it at the crosses. He knew they were not empty, for the birds were fluttering about them; and he thought how, as like as not, just such another vagabond as himself had been mounted on one of them; and he muttered: 'If it were hanging or bow-stringing, or stoning or beheading, it would be bad enough. But to have the birds pecking your eyes and the wolves eating your feet! I would that the red wind of the Druids had withered in his cradle the soldier of Dathi, who brought the tree of death out of barbarous lands, or that the lightning, when it smote Dathi at the foot of the mountain, had smitten him also, or that his grave had been dug by the green-haired and green-toothed mer-rows deep at the roots of the deep sea.'

While he spoke, he shivered from head to foot, and the sweat came out upon his face, and he knew not why, for he had looked upon many crosses. He passed over two hills and under the battlemented gate, and then round by a left-hand way to the door of the Abbey. It was studded with great nails, and when he knocked at it he roused the lay brother who was the porter, and of him he asked a place in the guest-house. Then the lay brother took a glowing turf on a shovel, and led the way to a big and naked outhouse strewn with very dirty rushes; and lighted a rush-candle fixed between two of the stones of the wall, and set the glowing turf upon the hearth and gave him two unlighted sods and a wisp of straw, and showed him a blanket hanging from a nail, and a shelf with a loaf of bread and a jug of water, and a tub in a far corner. Then the lay brother left him and went back to his place by the door. And Cumhal the son of Cormac began to blow upon the glowing turf that he might light the two sods and the wisp of straw; but the sods and the straw would not light, for they were damp. So he took off his pointed shoes, and drew the tub out of the corner with the thought of washing the dust of the highway from his feet; but the water was so dirty that he could not see the bottom. He was very hungry, for he had not eaten all that day, so he did not waste much anger upon the tub, but took up the black loaf, and bit into it, and then spat out the bite, for the bread was hard and mouldy. Still he did not give way to his anger, for he had not drunken these many hours; having a hope of heath beer or wine at his day's end, he had left the brooks untasted, to make his supper the more delightful. Now he put the jug to his lips, but he flung it from him straightway, for the water was bitter and ill-smelling. Then he gave the jug a kick, so that it broke against the opposite wall, and he took down the blanket to wrap it about him for the night. But no sooner did he touch it than it was alive with skipping fleas. At this, beside himself with anger, he rushed to the door of the guest-house, but the lay brother, being well accustomed to such outcries, had locked it on the outside; so he emptied the tub and began to beat the door with it, till the lay brother came to the door and asked what ailed him, and why he woke him out of sleep. 'What ails me!' shouted Cumhal; 'are not the sods as wet as the sands of the Three Rosses? and are not the fleas in the blanket as many as the waves of the sea and as lively? and is not the bread as hard as the heart of a lay brother who has forgotten God? and is not the water in the jug as bitter and as ill-smelling as his soul? and is not the foot-water the colour that shall be upon him when he has been charred in the Undying Fires?' The lay brother saw that the lock was fast, and went back to his niche, for he was too sleepy to talk with comfort. And Cumhal went on beating at the door, and presently he heard the lay brother's foot once more, and cried out at him, 'O cowardly and tyrannous race of monks, persecutors of the bard and the gleeman, haters of life and joy! O race that does not draw the sword and tell the truth! O race that melts the bones of the people with cowardice and with deceit!'

'Gleeman,' said the lay brother, 'I also make rhymes; I make many while I sit in my niche by the door, and I sorrow to hear the bards railing upon the monks. Brother, I would sleep, and therefore I make known to you that it is the head of the monastery, our gracious abbot, who orders all things concerning the lodging of travellers.'

'You may sleep,' said Cumhal, 'I will sing a bard's curse on the abbot.' And he set the tub upside down under the window, and stood upon it, and began to sing in a very loud voice. The singing awoke the abbot, so that he sat up in bed and blew a silver whistle until the lay brother came to him. 'I cannot get a wink of sleep with that noise,' said the abbot. 'What is happening?'

'It is a gleeman,' said the lay brother, 'who complains of the sods, of the bread, of the water in the jug, of the foot-water, and of the blanket. And now he is singing a bard's curse upon you, O brother abbot, and upon your father and your mother, and your grandfather and your grandmother, and upon all your relations.'

'Is he cursing in rhyme?'

'He is cursing in rhyme, and with two assonances in every line of his curse.'

The abbot pulled his night-cap off and crumpled it in his hands, and the circular grey patch of hair in the middle of his bald head looked like the cairn upon Knocknarea, for in Connaught they had not yet abandoned the ancient tonsure. 'Unless we do somewhat,' he said, 'he will teach his curses to the children in the street, and the girls spinning at the doors, and to the robbers upon Ben Bulben.'

'Shall I go, then,' said the other, 'and give him dry sods, a fresh loaf, clean water in a jug, clean foot-water, and a new blanket, and make him swear by the blessed Saint Benignus, and by the sun and moon, that no bond be lacking, not to tell his rhymes to the children in the street, and the girls spinning at the doors, and the robbers upon Ben Bulben?'

'Neither our Blessed Patron nor the sun and moon would avail at all,' said the abbot; 'for tomorrow or the next day the mood to curse would come upon him, or a pride in those rhymes would move him, and he would teach his lines to the children, and the girls, and the robbers. Or else he would tell another of his craft how he fared in the guest-house, and he in his turn would begin to curse, and my name would wither. For learn there is no steadfastness of purpose upon the roads, but only under roofs and between four walls. Therefore I bid you go and awaken Brother Kevin, Brother Dove, Brother Little Wolf, Brother Bald Patrick,

Brother Bald Brandon, Brother James, and Brother Peter. And they shall take the man, and bind him with ropes, and dip him in the river that he shall cease to sing. And in the morning, lest this but make him curse the louder, we will crucify him.'

'The crosses are all full,' said the lay brother.

'Then we must make another cross. If we do not make an end to him another will, for who can eat and sleep in peace while men like him are going about the world? We would stand shamed indeed before blessed Saint Benignus, and sour would be his face when he comes to judge us at the Last Day, were we to spare an enemy of his when we had him under our thumb! Brother, there is not one of these bards and gleemen who has not scattered his bastards through the five kingdoms, and if they slit a purse or a throat, and it is always one or the other, it never comes into their heads to confess and do penance. Can you name one that is not heathen in his heart, always longing after the Son of Lir, and Aengus, and Bridget, and the Dagda, and Dana the Mother, and all the false gods of the old days; always making poems in praise of those kings and queens of the demons, Finvaragh, whose home is under Cruachmaa, and Red Aodh of Cnocna-Sidhe, and Cleena of the Wave, and Aoibhell of the Grey Rock, and him they call Donn of the Vats of the Sea; and railing against God and Christ and the blessed Saints.' While he was speaking he crossed himself, and when he had finished he drew the nightcap over his ears to shut out the noise, and closed his eyes and composed himself to sleep.

The lay brother found Brother Kevin, Brother Dove, Brother Little Wolf, Brother Bald Patrick, Brother Bald Brandon, Brother James, and Brother Peter sitting up in bed, and he made them get up. Then they bound Cumhal, and they dragged him to the river, and they dipped him in it at the place which was afterwards called Buckley's Ford.

'Gleeman,' said the lay brother, as they led him back to the guest-house, 'why do you ever use the wit which God has given you to make blasphemous and immoral tales and verses? For such is the way of your craft. I have, indeed, many such tales and verses wellnigh by rote, and so I know that I speak true! And why do you praise with rhyme those demons, Finvaragh, Red Aodh, Cleena, Aoibhell and Donn? I, too, am a man of great wit and learning, but I ever glorify our gracious abbot, and Benignus our Patron, and the princes of the province. My soul is decent and orderly, but yours is like the wind among the salley gardens. I said what I could for you, being also a man of many thoughts, but who could help such a one as you?'

'Friend,' answered the gleeman, 'my soul is indeed like the wind, and it blows me to and fro, and up and down, and puts many things into my mind and out of my mind, and therefore am I called the Swift, Wild Horse.' And he spoke no more that night, for his teeth were chattering with the cold.

The abbot and the monks came to him in the morning, and bade him get ready to be crucified, and led him out of the guest-house. And while he still stood upon the step a flock of great grass-barnacles passed high above him with clanking cries. He lifted his arms to them and said, 'O great grass-barnacles, tarry a little, and mayhap my soul will travel with you to the waste places of the shore and to the ungovernable sea!' At the gate a crowd of beggars gathered about them, being come there to beg from any traveller or pilgrim who might have spent the night in the guest-house. The abbot and the monks led the gleeman to a place in the woods at some distance, where many straight young trees were growing, and they made him cut one down and fashion it to the right length, while the beggars stood round them in a ring, talking and gesticulating. The abbot then bade him cut off another and shorter piece of wood, and nail it upon the first. So there was his cross for him, and they put it upon his shoulder, for his cruci-fixion was to be on the top of the hill where the others were. A half-mile on the way he asked them to stop and see him juggle for them; for he knew, he said, all the tricks of Aengus and Subtle-hearted. The old monks were for pressing on, but the young monks would see him: so he did many wonders for them, even to the drawing of live frogs out of his ears. But after a while they turned on him, and said his tricks were dull and a little unholy, and set the cross on his shoulders again. Another half-mile on the way and he asked them to stop and hear him jest for them, for he knew, he said, all the jests of Conan the Bald, upon whose back a sheep's wool grew. And the young monks, when they had heard his merry tales, again bade him take up his cross, for it ill became them to listen to such follies. Another half-mile on the way, he asked them to stop and hear him sing the story of White-breasted Deirdre, and how she endured many sorrows, and how the sons of Usna died to serve her. And the young monks were mad to hear him, but when he had ended they grew angry, and beat him for waking forgotten longings in their hearts. So they set the cross upon his back and hurried him to the hill.

When he was come to the top, they took the cross from him, and began to dig a hole for it to stand in, while the beggars gathered round, and talked among themselves. 'I ask a favour before I die,' says Cumhal.

'We will grant you no more delays,' says the abbot.

'I ask no more delays, for I have drawn the sword, and told the truth, and lived my dream, and am content.'

'Would you, then, confess?'

'By sun and moon, not I; I ask but to be let eat the food I carry in my wallet. I carry food in my wallet whenever I go upon a journey, but I do not taste of it unless I am wellnigh starved. I have not eaten now these two days.'

'You may eat, then,' says the abbot, and he turned to help the monks dig the hole.

The gleeman took a loaf and some strips of cold fried bacon out of his wallet and laid them upon the ground. 'I will give a tithe to the poor,' says he, and he cut a tenth part from the loaf and the bacon. 'Who among you is the poorest?' And thereupon was a great clamour, for the beggars began the history of their sorrows and their poverty, and their yellow faces swayed like Gara Lough when the floods have filled it with water from the bogs.

He listened for a little, and, says he, 'I am myself the poorest, for I have travelled the bare road, and by the edges of the sea; and the tattered doublet of parti-coloured cloth upon my back and the torn pointed shoes upon my feet have ever irked me, because of the towered city full of noble raiment which was in my heart. And I have been the more alone upon the roads and by the sea because I heard in my heart the rustling of the rose-bordered dress of her who is more subtle than Aengus the Subtle-hearted, and more full of the beauty of laughter than Conan the Bald, and more full of the wisdom of tears than White-breasted Deirdre, and more lovely than a bursting dawn to them that are lost in the darkness. Therefore, I award the tithe to myself; but yet, because I am done with all things, I give it unto you.'

So he flung the bread and the strips of bacon among the beggars, and they fought with many cries until the last scrap was eaten. But meanwhile the monks nailed the gleeman to his cross, and set it upright in the hole, and shovelled the earth into the hole, and trampled it level and hard. So then they went away, but the beggars stayed on, sitting round the cross. But when the sun was sinking, they also got up to go, for the air was getting chilly. And as soon as they had gone a little way, the wolves, who had been showing themselves on the edge of a neighbouring coppice, came nearer, and the birds wheeled closer and closer. 'Stay, outcasts, yet a little while,' the crucified one called in a weak voice to the beggars, 'and keep the beasts and the birds from me.' But the beggars were angry because he had called them outcasts, so they threw stones and mud at him, and one that had a child held it up before his eyes and said that he was its father, and cursed him, and thereupon they left him. Then the wolves gathered at the foot of the cross, and the birds flew lower and lower. And presently the birds lighted all at once upon his head and arms and shoulders, and began to peck at him, and the wolves began to eat his feet. 'Outcasts,' he moaned, 'have you all turned against the outcast?'

W. B. YEATS

William Butler Yeats was born in Sandymount, County Dublin, Ireland in 1865. He spent his childhood in Country Sligo, and was educated in London, but returned to Dublin at the age of fifteen with the intention of pursuing painting. However, he quickly discovered he preferred poetry, and became involved with the Celtic Revival, an Irish movement resisting the cultural influence of English rule during the Victorian period. Throughout his life, much of Yeats' work was included by Irish mythology and folklore, as well as various types of mysticism and occultism.

Yeats' first verse play, *Mosada,* was published in 1886. Over the next few years, he continued to write, and mingled with many literary luminaries of the day, such as George Bernard Shaw and Oscar Wilde. His *The Wanderings of Usheen and other Poems* was published in 1889, and brought him some attention from critics. In the late 1890s, he became involved with The Abbey Theatre – the institution which propelled him to fame and success. As its chief playwright, Yeats staged a number of his best-remembered productions during the years up to 1911, including *The Countess Cathleen* (1892), *The Land of Heart's Desire* (1894) and *The King's Threshold* (1904).

From 1910 onwards, Yeats focussed more on poetry. The collections of lyrical poetry he penned during his last decades - such as *The Wild Swans at Coole* (1919), *Michael Robartes and the Dancer* (1921), *The Tower* (1928), *The Winding Stair and Other Poems* (1933), and *Last Poems and Plays* (1940) – made him one of the most acclaimed and influential poets in Europe. In 1923, he was awarded the Nobel Prize for Literature. He died in 1939, aged 73, and is now regarded as one of the twentieth century's key English language poets, and a master of the traditional forms.